THE DAY YOU BEGIN

JACQUELINE WOODSON

illustrated by RAFAEL LÓPEZ

NANCY PAULSEN BOOKS

NANCY PAULSEN BOOKS
an imprint of Penguin Random House LLC
375 Hudson Street
New York, NY 10014

Library of Congress Cataloging-in-Publication Data is available upon request.

Manufactured in China by RR Donnelley Asia Printing Solutions Ltd.
ISBN 9780399246531
17

Design by Jaclyn Reyes.
Text set in Siseriff LT Std.
The illustrations were created with a combination of acrylic paint on wood, pen and ink, pencil, and watercolors, and put together digitally in Photoshop.

For Siya, Nell, and Josie —J.W.

To Santiago, Moon whisperer —R.L.

There will be times when you walk into a room
and no one there is quite like you.

Maybe it will be your skin, your clothes, or the curl of your hair.

There will be times when no one understands the way
words curl from your mouth,
the beautiful language of the country you left behind.
My name is Rigoberto. We just moved here from Venezuela.

And because they don't understand, the classroom will fill
with laughter until the teacher quiets everyone.

Rigoberto. From Venezuela, your teacher says so soft and beautifully that your name and homeland sound like
flowers blooming the first bright notes

of a song.

There will be times when the words don't come.
Your own voice, once huge, now smaller
when the teacher asks *What did you do last summer?*
Tell the class your story.

We went to France, Chayla says.

These shells came from a beach in Maine.
A boy named Jonathan holds out a jar
filled with tiny shells so fragile,
they look like they'll turn to dust
in your own untraveled hands.

My whole family went to India.
Spain!
South Carolina!
Each souvenir a small triumph
of a journey.
Their travels going on and on.

And as you stand in front of that room, you can only remember
how the heat waved
as it lifted off the curb,
and your days spent at home
caring for your little sister,
who made you laugh out loud and hugged you hard
at naptime. You can only remember the books you kept on reading
long after she had fallen
to sleep.

And in that room, where no one else is quite like you, you'll look down
at your own empty hands and wonder *What good is this*
when other students were flying
and sailing and
going somewhere.

There will be times when the lunch your mother packed for you
is too strange or
too unfamiliar for others
to love as you do.

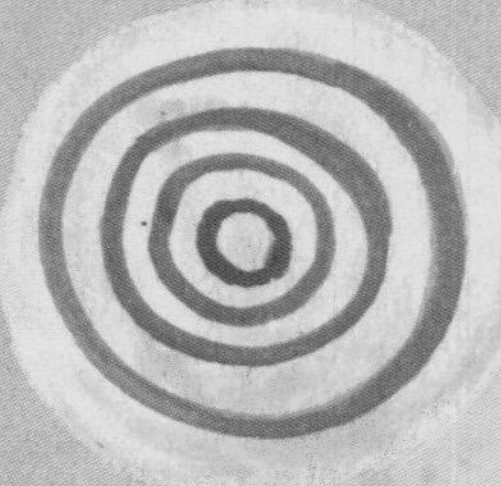

When even your own friend Nadja
will wrinkle her nose and say *What's in there, anyway?*
And you'll wonder how she doesn't see the rice
beneath the meat and kimchi.
You'll wonder why she doesn't remember
that rice is the most popular food in the world.

There will be times when the climbing bars are too high,
the run is too fast and far,
the game isn't one you can ever really play.

I don't want him on our team.
You can watch.
Maybe you can have a turn later.

There will be times when the world feels like a place
that you're standing all the way
outside of . . .

And all that stands beside you *is*
your own brave self—
steady as steel and ready
even though you don't yet know
what you're ready for.

There will be times when you walk into a room
and no one there is quite like you until the day you begin

to share your stories. *My name is Angelina and*
I spent my whole summer with my little sister,
you tell the class, your voice
stronger than it was a minute ago,
reading books and telling stories and
even though we were right on our block it was like
we got to go EVERYWHERE.

Your name is like my sister's, Rigoberto says.
Her name is Angelina, too.

And all at once, in the room where no one else is quite like you,
the world opens itself up a little wider
to make some space for you.

This is the day you begin

to find the places inside
your laughter and your lunches,
your books, your travel and your stories,

where every new friend has something
a little like you—and something else
so fabulously not quite like you
at all.